Disney's
My Very First Winnie the Pooh™

Tigger Takes Over

Written by
Agnes Sumner

Illustrated by
Kim Raymond

SCHOLASTIC INC.

New York Toronto London Auckland Sydney
Mexico City New Delhi Hong Kong Buenos Aires

Published by Scholastic Inc., 90 Old Sherman Turnpike, Danbury, CT 06816
by arrangement with Disney Licensed Publishing.

SCHOLASTIC and associated logos are trademarks
and/or registered trademarks of Scholastic Inc.

ISBN 0-7172-8963-X

Printed in the U.S.A.

One day, Tigger got bored bouncing by himself in the Hundred-Acre Wood. So he decided to bounce over to Kanga and Roo's.

Roo was outside playing.

"Hiya, kid," Tigger called. "How's about me and you scaring us up some fun?"

"Can I, Mama? Please?" Roo begged, turning to Kanga.

Kanga smiled. "Well, I do have some things I need to do this afternoon."

"Tigger, dear, could you keep an eye on Roo for a few hours?" asked Kanga.

Tigger blushed, just like he always did when Kanga called him 'dear.' "Aw, shucks, Mrs. Kanga. I'd love to hang out with the kid."

"Thank you, dear," said Kanga, and Tigger blushed again. "Now, Roo," Kanga went on, "I'm putting Tigger in charge, so stay with him and listen to what he says."

"Don't worry, Mama," cried Roo. "I'll be on my bestest behavior!" And he and Tigger bounced off, shouting, "T-T-F-N, Ta-Ta For Now!"

"*H*oo-hoo-hoo!" Tigger exclaimed. "Did you hear that, Little Buddy? I'm *in charge!*" Tigger bounced an extra-springy bounce. "I say we play *Simon Says*, only we'll call it *Tigger Says*, since I'm *in charge* and all."

"I love *Simon*—I mean, *Tigger Says!*" replied Roo. "Let's play!"

And so the two friends played— touching their noses and wiggling their tails as Tigger called out the orders.

"I'm really gettin' the hang of this *being in charge* stuff," Tigger proclaimed.

Just then, Pooh and Piglet happened by. They were both carrying baskets full of haycorns that they had collected for Piglet.

"Hiya, Buddy Boys!" shouted Tigger, knocking haycorns every which way. "We're playing *Tigger Says*. Come stand over here," he added, pulling Pooh and Piglet over next to Roo. "Now just do what Tigger Says."

"B-but Tigger, we h-have to finish gathering and storing these haycorns," protested Piglet.

"Tigger Says 'nonsense!'" replied Tigger.

Soon, all four friends were covering their eyes, stamping their feet, and rubbing their tummies.

But when Pooh rubbed his tummy, he noticed it was rumbly. So he and Piglet decided to go home for a smackerel of something to eat.

"But Tigger didn't Say!" insisted Tigger, trying to get his friends to stay. "Besides, Kanga says I'm *in charge*!"

Pooh just shook his head. "Right now, *my tummy's* in charge, and it says I have to give it some honey."

And with that, he and Piglet picked up what was left of their haycorns and went.

"Well, looks like it's just you and me again, kid," said Tigger to Roo. "Tigger Says let's go see what Eeyore's up to, an' we have to bounce all the way there!" So the two friends bounced over to Eeyore's place.

"Whatcha doin' there, Donkey Boy?" Tigger asked Eeyore.

"Not that it matters, but I'm rebuilding my house," answered Eeyore. "The wind blew it over. Again."

"Well, no wonder it keeps blowin' over. You're doin' it all wrong," Tigger replied. "Lucky for you, me and the kid happened by. I'll take charge and show you how it's done."

Tigger pushed Eeyore aside and took over rebuilding the house. Sticks flew everywhere.

"Ta-da!" cried Tigger when he had finished. "Whaddya think?"

Eeyore looked sadly at his new house. "It's okay, I suppose," he mumbled. "If you don't mind sleeping outdoors. Which I *do*, as a matter of fact," Eeyore added to himself.

"Well, I say it's fantastickal," cried Tigger. "I'm just glad I could help out my buddy, Buddy Boy. Now me and Roo are gonna go and see if Rabbit has anything that I can be in charge of."

Roo and Tigger bounced on over to Rabbit's house. Rabbit was in his garden.

"Helloo, Long Ears," Tigger called out.

"Helloo, Long Ears," Roo repeated.

"Oh, hello. Thank goodness you didn't bounce me today," said Rabbit. "I have so much work to do that even one bounce would have seriously delayed me."

Rabbit went back to patting the soil down carefully. Then he gently watered each small mound of dirt.

"No wonders you have lotsa work," said Tigger. "You're goin' about it all wrong. With me in charge, it'll be done lickety-split."

Tigger grabbed the seeds, scattered them every which way, and bounced them into the ground. Then he showered them with the hose until Rabbit's entire garden was one giant mud puddle.

"Tigger, what are you doing?!" cried Rabbit, running around in circles and pulling at his ears. "My garden! My precious garden!"

"Why, thank you," Tigger stated proudly. "It *is* rather wunnerful work, if I do say so myself."

"No, no, no!" shouted Rabbit. "You've *ruined* my garden. Just go away, Tigger!"

"Uh-oh, Tigger," Roo said. "You're in trouble."

"Me? In trouble? That's ridickerous," Tigger replied. "Tiggers never get in trouble!"

"They do *this* time!" yelled Rabbit.

"It's impossibibble for me to be in trouble 'cause I'm *in charge*!" Tigger said.

"Says *who*?" Rabbit shouted.

"Mrs. Kanga says, that's who!" announced Tigger, crossing his arms triumphantly.

"Mama put Tigger in charge," agreed Roo, nodding his head.

Just then, Kanga came looking for Roo. "Oh, my! What is all the arguing about?" she asked.

"Tigger has ruined my garden," wailed Rabbit.

"Tigger! Is this true?" asked Kanga.

"Well, Rabbit was planting all wrong. I just showed him how he should be doing it," Tigger explained. "Besides, you *said* I was in charge."

"But, Tigger, I only put you in charge of keeping Roo out of trouble. Being in charge doesn't mean bossing everyone around, dear."

"I guess I got a little carried away," said Tigger, blushing. "You know how us tiggers can be," he said. "I'm sorry, Mrs. Kanga."

"You should really be apologizing to Rabbit," corrected Kanga, gently.

Tigger thought for a moment. "You're right. I don't partickerlerly like it when Rabbit tries to tell me how to bounce," he replied. Tigger looked at Rabbit. "Sorry, Long Ears."

"'Sorry'?! *Sorry's* not going to fix my garden!" screeched Rabbit.

"Oh, all right, I'll help fix your garden," agreed Tigger. "I'll come back tomorrow, when it's dry. I'll even do it your way. But first I gotta see somebody else." And before anyone could say a word, away he bounced.

Tigger paid a visit on Eeyore. "I'm sorry about your house, Ol' Buddy, an' I came to help you rebuild it."

"Are you in charge again?" Eeyore asked, suspiciously.

"Nope. You tell me whatcha want, an' I'll do it!" replied Tigger.

So they worked side by side. When they were done, Eeyore stepped into the house to try it on for size.

"This is one Eeyorgeous house, Donkey Boy!" exclaimed Tigger.

Eeyore nodded with a shy smile.

*E*arly next morning, Tigger bounded out into the Hundred-Acre Wood. He had important things to do.

Tigger found a basket and filled it with a whole bunch of haycorns. Then, he bounced them over to Piglet's house. Piglet and Pooh were sitting outside in the sun.

"These are for you 'cause I'm sorry," explained Tigger. "This being in charge stuff isn't as easy as I thought. Now, if you guyses don't mind, I'm gonna bounce on outta here!—T-T-F-N, Ta-Ta For Now!" Tigger called, bouncing away.

Tigger spent the rest of the day helping Rabbit re-organize his garden. That evening, Kanga invited Tigger over to have a special supper with Roo.

"I am so proud of you for cooperating with your friends, Tigger, dear!" said Kanga.

"Yeah?" Tigger's nose blushed extra pink. "An' ya know what, Mrs. Kanga?" he blurted. "Co-paperating is lots funner than bossing, too! Hoo-hoo-hoo!"